where the birdies and trees dilly-dally,

lives happy Little Pine
with big old trees.

To Miyun,
my cute little nephew.

Published by Nirdesha Munasinghe.
https://www.facebook.com/NirdeshaArt
https://www.youtube.com/user/nirdesha
Instagram: @nirdesha_art

Happy Little Pine

Nirdesha Munasinghe

Over the hills, in a green valley,

She plays
in the sun

and sways
in the breeze.

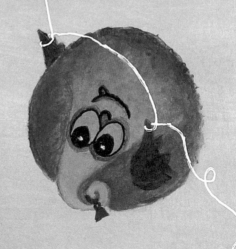

She's a beautiful green,
the cutest pine.
She has big rooty feet
and a curly top so fine.

A man comes down...

from the hills one day.

He digs up Little Pine
and takes her...

away.

The man is happy.
He's found the one!
Perfect Christmas tree
for his little son.

But the big trees are sad.
They cry, and they sigh.

"Let's leave the valley,
tell our home goodbye."

The trees bid farewell
with a sad little song.
It echos through the valley
like a sorrowful moan.
The valley grows empty
as the trees leave
their home.

Only the man stands tall
on the hill all alone.

Gone are the trees,
the streams,
the birdies,

all the
little critters,
and the fluffy
little bunnies.

Gone, gone, gone!
But not for too long.

Little Pine returns
to where she belongs.

The big trees come back.

What a happy day!

The birdies and bunnies
are making their way.
The stream is flowing.
A cool breeze is blowing,
making Little Pine's
curly top sway.

Happy Little Pine plays
with her friends.

She hopes that the party of trees never ends.

The man joins in
with the fun of the day.
He swears not to take
Little Pine away.

Never again.

Made in the USA
Las Vegas, NV
26 October 2021